Christmas Eve

Suçie Stevenson

A PICTURE YEARLING BOOK

Published by
Dell Publishing
a division of
Bantam Doubleday Dell Publishing Group, Inc.
666 Fifth Avenue
New York, New York 10103

The trademark Yearling® is registered in the U.S. Patent and
Trademark Office.

The trademark Dell® is registered in the U.S. Patent and
Trademark Office.

ISBN: 0-440-40729-X

Reprinted by arrangement with The Putnam & Grosset Book
Group

Printed in the United States of America
November 1992
10 9 8 7 6 5 4 3 2 1

For MA and POP

"Christmas cookies to decorate!" cried Mama.
"My favorite!" said Elly.
"You girls come make these cookies beautiful," said Mama,
"while I change Mae."

"I can do it all by myself, just fine!" said Elly.
"Let Violet help, dear," said Mama.
"Not Violet!" moaned Elly.

"OK. We have nuts, and raisins, and colored sprinkles..."
  said Elly.

"Sprinkles – Tinkles," sang Violet.

"Way too many sprinkles, Violet!" said Elly. "You're
  throwing them."

"Sprinkles – Linkles – Prinkles," sang Violet.

"And, do you *have* to sing?" asked Elly.

"That's supposed to be a gingerbread man, you know," said Elly.

Violet poked in some more raisins.

"Enough raisins!" said Elly, "and quit mashing him!"

"This is what he's *supposed* to look like," said Elly, "see, mine's perfect."

"Mine's perfect," Violet said, adding a raisin.

"I'll put these in the oven to bake," said Mama. "Why don't you see if the tree needs watering in the Christmas Room and hang up your stockings for Santa Claus? You can take Mae."

Elly hung up her sock with her name on it and little Mae's with her name on it.

Violet hung up her tights with her name on them.

"No fair!" yelled Elly.

"Girls, Girls, why don't you go outside for awhile," said
Mama, "while I give Mae her bottle."

"I just know I'm going to finally get a pony for Christmas," said Elly, as they crunched through the snow.
"See?" said Elly. "Look, here's a bale of hay."
"Nope, that's not for horses," said Violet. "That's to put on ice."

"Look, here in the garage," said Elly, "a pail of oats."
"Nope, that's bird food," said Violet.
"Since when do you know everything!" said Elly.

"I'm going to get a baby doll in a lace nightgown for Christmas," said Violet. "Santa Claus comes tonight, right, Elly?"
"Maybe." said Elly.
"MAYBE?" cried Violet.

"It depends," said Elly.

"I'll leave lots of cookies for the reindeer," said Violet.

"He could forget you, maybe," said Elly. "Santa Claus
probably doesn't remember *you*."

All the stockings were hung on the fireplace in the
Christmas Room.
Elly and Violet kept coming back to look at them all day.

"I bet Mama and Papa would love their own stockings! We can make them as a surprise," said Elly. "We can pretend they're from Santa Claus."

"YAY!" cried Violet. "Stockings – Tockings for everybody! . Mama has big feet," said Violet, "so does Papa."

"We'll use our socks," said Elly.

They raced around the house collecting things to wrap for each stocking.

PAPA'S STOCKING

Christmas Cookies

A Red Truck

Candy Canes off the Tree

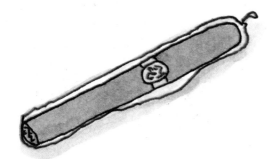

A Cigar from Papa's Box

An Orange for the Toe

"OK. Stuff them up," said Elly.

MAMA'S STOCKING

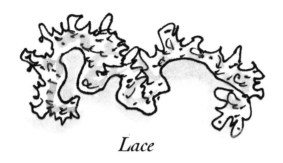

Lace

Scented Soap

Grandma's Fake Earrings

Violet's Teddy Bear

An Orange for the Toe

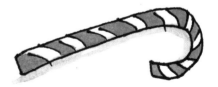

Candy Cane off the Tree

"These are good," said Violet.
"Let's hide them under the bed," said Elly.

"Now, the best part," said Elly. "I'm going to make Mama
 and Papa their big present."
"I want to," said Violet.
"It's going to be really good, just from me," said Elly.
"Make your own present, Violet!"

"I don't know how yet," sobbed Violet.
"OK. OK. Shhh!" said Elly. "I guess you can help me. We'll
 do it together."

Elly sent Violet to get tape, purple tissue paper, gold gum
stars, sea rocks, sticks and glue, scissors and paint.
Elly took out her special piece of driftwood.

"Rocks? What are we making?" asked Violet.
"*I'm* making a statue of us. They'll love it," said Elly.
"You can use my blue mussel shells for ears," said Violet.
"Thanks, Violet," said Elly, "that will be perfect."

"In that statue, where am I?" asked Violet.
"This is you." said Elly.
"That's not me," said Violet, "that looks like *you*."

"I know how to wrap," said Violet. They put the statue in a
  shoe box.
"Wrap it – Bap it – Snap it," sang Violet. She crumpled up
  tissue paper and licked and licked gold stars.

"Violet, take that tape off your ears," said Elly.
"The tape is stuck!" cried Violet. Elly unwrapped her.
"Ow! Ow!" cried Violet.
"You have stars stuck all over you," said Elly.

"They'll be so surprised," said Violet.
"I can't wait for tomorrow," said Elly. They put the shoe
box under the bed, too.

"Time for bed, girls," said Mama.

"Sweet dreams," said Papa.

"I want Christmas now!" whispered Violet.

"Christmas Eve always comes first," whispered Elly.

"Night, Mama," called Elly.

"Night, Papa," called Violet.

"Are you sleeping?" asked Elly.

"I don't think so," said Violet.

"Can you sneak?" asked Elly.

"Squeak, squeak, squeak," said Violet.

"No, silly! Let's sneak out. I know where Papa keeps the cards. We can play cards all night while we wait for Santa to come."

"GO FISH!" yelled Violet.
"Shhh! Keep it down," said Elly.
"GO FISH!" yelled Violet.
"That's what you say *every* time! You don't even know how
  to read cards," hissed Elly.

"Go Fish," whispered Violet.
"DON'T BEND THE CARDS!" yelled Elly.
"GO FISH," yelled Violet.
"CHILDREN!" said Mama. "Are you awake?"
"I knew it, Violet, this is all your fault!" said Elly.

At dawn the sky turned pink.
Violet wiggled her finger in Elly's ear. "Guess what?"
she asked.
"What?!" yelled Elly.
"IT'S CHRISTMAS!" yelled Violet. "Merry Christmas,"
she whispered.

"Merry Christmas!!" yelled Elly.
"Let's go wake up everyone!" said Elly.

"Santa Claus came! We found these upstairs for you,"
they said.
"A stocking for me?" asked Mama.
"A stocking," said Papa, "my favorite!"

"Time for the Christmas Room," said Papa, as he led the way. Elly and Violet each carried an end of the special shoe box as they scampered down the stairs.

"Santy – Claus! Panty – Claus," sang the girls together, "Christmas – Nissmus – didn't miss us."